Published by:

Name This Pig
Burnley, Victoria, 3121
Australia
web: preemietheexplorer.com
email: info@preemietheexplorer.com

National Library of Australia Cataloguing-in-Publication entry:
Author:      Haggart, Rohan.
Title:       Preemie the explorer: The little rocket who took off too
             soon / by Rohan Haggart ; illustrated by Andrew Hopgood.

ISBN:        978-0-9873533-0-6 (pbk)

Target Audience: Primary school age.

Subjects:    Premature infants--Juvenile fiction.
             Rockets (Aeronautics)--Juvenile fiction.
             Bullying--Juvenile fiction.

Dewey Number: A823.4

Seventeen original illustrations by Andrew Hopgood are included in the book. Other illustrations were added by Rohan Haggart, using layers from Andrew's original illustrations either by themselves or in composite pictures.

Design by Rohan Haggart.

*Preemie the Explorer: The Little Rocket Who Took Off Too Soon* is designed to help children understand that being different and confronting social challenges can be like a wild, exciting ride through space!

# The Little Rocket
# Who Took Off Too Soon

## Written By Rohan Haggart
## Illustrated by Andrew Hopgood

Name This Pig
Melbourne, Australia
www.preemietheexplorer.com

# Acknowledgements

Sincere thanks to the following people for their help during the writing of "*Preemie the Explorer: The Little Rocket Who Took Off Too Soon*":  Dr. Carly Molloy (founder of *www.preemiehelp.com*), Laura Duncan, Timon Duncan, Tas Gray, Sally Odgers, Tania McCartney, Chris Grigoropoulos, Candace Borg, Lee-Anne Walker, Debby Hirst, Keala Burns, and Louisa O'Toole.

Special thanks to Andrew Hopgood for drawing such beautiful illustrations. Your virtuosity is stunning, and your approach to the collaborative process made working with you an effortless joy.

There are six American spellings in the book which should be noted for Australian readers.

The words are:
1. moldy (mouldy)
2. colors (colours)
3. favorite (favourite)
4. meters (metres)
5. realized (realised)
6. realizing (realising)

# Chapter 1

In the building yard of Mama Spacecraft, a brand new rocket was being built. The rocket capsule stood attached to his launching tower while two builders, Googie and Tad, connected his shiny new engines.

"Am I a rocket yet?" asked the capsule for the twenty-eighth time.

"Not yet," replied Tad, wiping sweat from his brow.

"Aww, how much longer?"

"Three more bolts and your engines will be attached," said Tad.

The capsule squealed with excitement.

*"I'm so close to rockethood, I can smell it,"* he said, forgetting that rockets don't have noses.

Tad smiled as he carefully tightened the last engine bolt.

Googie giggled as she watched Tad casually toss his spanner into the tool box and sit down.

"Now?" repeated the capsule, trembling with excitement. "Am I a rocket now?"

After a long pause, Tad finally answered.

*"Now you are a rocket!"*

# Chapter 2

"I'm a rocket. I can fly. Time to zoom across the sky!" shrieked the rocket with delight.

"It's not quite time for take-off yet," said Tad.

"You still have a lot of growing to do," added Googie with a loving smile.

"Watch out, Milky Way, here I come!" yelled the rocket. "Look at my lights and buttons and computers. I'm more fun than a video game...."

The rocket babbled on. He was so excited about having his engines connected, he hadn't listened carefully to what his builders had said.

"You're not ready for the Milky Way," Tad interrupted abruptly.

The rocket stopped babbling.

"You're kidding me?" he pleaded.

**"The universe is calling, 'fly to me rocket, take off and fly to me!'"**

The builders laughed as the rocket impersonated the voice of the universe.

"Oh, baby," said Googie, giving the rocket a gentle hug, "we haven't connected all your computers yet, so you might get lost."

"Don't forget about his outer shell and turbo thrusters," said Tad, winking at Googie.

"Outer shell? Turbo thrusters? You mean there's going to be more of me?" asked the rocket.

"That's right," answered Tad, pointing to a picture of how the rocket would look when he was finished.

*"Your outer shell and turbo thrusters will make you twice as big, three times as fast, and four times as strong."*

*The little rocket swelled with pride. "I am going to be awesome!" he said.*

Googie smiled. "You're going to be our masterpiece," she replied.

Feelings of happiness filled the little rocket and his lights lit up all at once.

"We need a name for you," said Tad.

"Hmmm, what should we call a beautiful baby who dreams of leaving his launching platform before he's ready?" asked Googie.

The rocket waited eagerly for a suggestion.

MAMA SPACECRAFT

"Dreamy Preemie?" suggested Tad.

"What's a preemie?" asked the little rocket.

**"A preemie is a brand new creature who is so excited about exploring the universe, he just can't wait until he's finished being made," answered Googie.**

"That's me!" said the little rocket. "Call me, Preemie the Explorer!"

"Preemie the Explorer," repeated Tad.

"A name and a title," said Googie. "Very fancy!"

"Excellent!" they all said together.

"So, when can I take off and explore?" asked Preemie.

"When you're perfect," said Googie, "we will paint

across your window in all the glorious colors of the rainbow."

# Chapter 3

"Goodbye, Preemie the Explorer," said Tad as the two builders left work for the day.

"See you tomorrow," added Googie, blowing Preemie a kiss.

Preemie didn't hear them. He was already lost in a daydream, imagining himself soaring through the endless sky. He thought about the strange and wonderful planets he would visit, the fun spaceships and rockets he would meet, and, most of all, the way he would fly smoother and faster than any other spacecraft in the universe.

Preemie's daydream was interrupted by the sound of thunder. He looked up and saw dark storm clouds approaching like giant whales in the sky. Preemie closed one eye as thick raindrops splashed onto his cabin windows, and a cold wind whistled around his engines.

"Is anybody here?" he yelled.

One of the building yard gates squeaked as it swung open in the wind, but there were no people or spacecraft in sight.

The clouds grew darker, the wind howled harder, the rain fell heavier, and Preemie shivered until his nuts and bolts clattered.

*Suddenly, a jagged barb of lightning shot across the dark sky and thunder cracked so loudly that Preemie shut his other eye, hoping the sky wouldn't collapse on top of him. The little rocket was scared and his cabin lights flickered uncontrollably.*

# Chapter 4

Nearby, two children, named Veronica and Jeffy, were struggling to carry their little sister, Lola, through the rain and puddles. When they saw Mama Spacecraft's gate wide open and Preemie standing alone in the yard, they scurried inside the rocket's capsule for shelter.

*"Sweet ship!" said Jeffy, as the children made themselves at home.*

Preemie's lights brightened and he silently listened for more compliments.

"I'm a movie star," announced Veronica, lounging on the couch in a fancy pose.

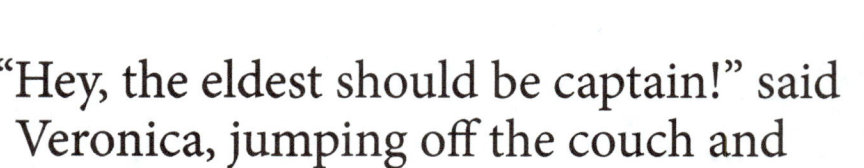

Lola giggled as she clicked and turned every switch and knob she could reach.

"I'm the captain of this rocket-ship," said Jeffy, spinning around in the captain's chair.

**It was so exciting, everyone forgot about the storm, including Preemie.**

"Hey, the eldest should be captain!" said Veronica, jumping off the couch and holding up ten fingers to indicate her age.

"Just because you're older doesn't mean you should get everything!" replied Jeffy, crossing his arms and sitting tight.

"I'm the smartest too!" said Veronica.

"Who says?" demanded Jeffy.

"See, if you don't even know it was me who just said that, I must be the smartest!" said Veronica with a smug smile.

Jeffy was used to being outsmarted by Veronica, but this time he had the prize safely underneath his bottom.

"Well, this is the captain's chair," said Jeffy, "and I'm in it!"

On the control panel was an orange button labelled:

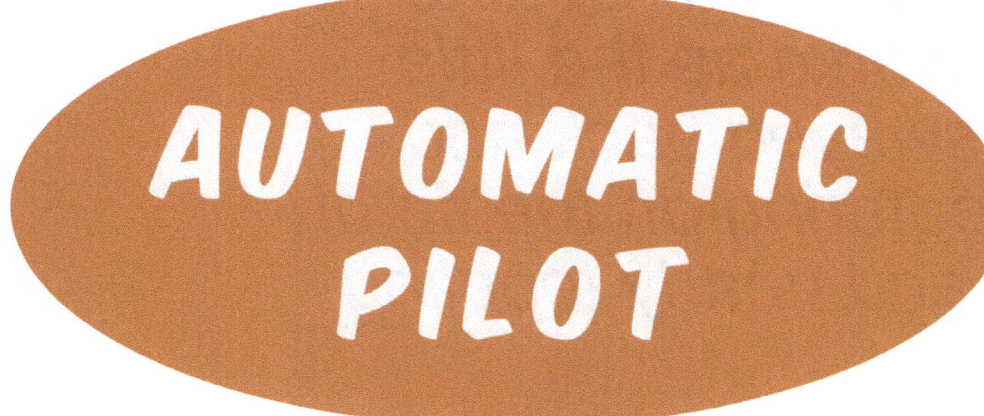

**AUTOMATIC PILOT**

Veronica pushed it. A surge of energy shot through Preemie's body. Some of his computers lit up as they engaged his engines, preparing him for flight.

*"A captain has to do more than just sit in a chair!"* said Veronica.

# Chapter 5

Preemie gasped. For the first time ever, he had the power to fly. Of course, he would never do it without permission from his builders, but he was excited to know he was finally able.

*Kaboom! A bolt of lightning smashed into the launching tower and snapped the support beams which were holding Preemie upright. Sparks flew like fireworks as the little rocket swayed back and forth, teetering on the tip of his tail and nearly toppling over.*

"Whoooooaaaahhhhh!" screamed the children as they fell about the cabin. Preemie tensed his engines as tightly as he could and just managed to remain standing.

The sky cracked with thunder again, this time so loudly the children couldn't hear their own screams. Preemie saw fear in their little eyes and, in a moment of panic, he activated the take off switch.

An automated countdown began:

# TEN, NINE, EIGHT....

"Quick, help me buckle Lola into her seat," Veronica said to Jeffy. When Lola was safely strapped in, Veronica hurried into the captain's chair.

# SEVEN, SIX, FIVE....

Jeffy grumbled as he climbed into the co-pilot's chair and fastened his seat belt.

"Ready for take off. Hurry up!" ordered Veronica, as Preemie continued to lurch from side to side with the howling wind.

# FOUR, THREE, TWO....

"Up and away!" yelled Jeffy.

# ONE....

# TAAAAAAKE OOOOOOFF!

Preemie jittered with fear and excitement. The children held their breath. The storm raged like an angry monster. But, the little rocket did not move.

Preemie strained his engines. They coughed and spluttered, then emitted just a single puff of smoke.

"Why isn't he taking off?" Veronica whispered loudly to Jeffy.

Jeffy shrugged.

"Ask him! You pressed the automatic-pilot button!" he said.

To the children's surprise, Preemie's voice came through speakers inside the cabin.

"Does anyone know how to fly?" he asked.

Jeffy and Veronica glared at each other with wide eyed terror.

Kapow! Another fork of lightning shot down from the sky like a giant burning spear. It exploded into Preemie's launching tower, smashing it to the ground.

"Heeeelp!" yelled Veronica and Jeffy over the roaring thunder.

*Without any time to think, Preemie's engines gushed with fire and smoke, and he rocketed into the sky.*

# Chapter 6

Preemie was soon cruising far above the storm clouds. He quickly forgot about the terrifying take-off, and began marvelling at the planets and stars which gleamed like glossy Christmas ornaments.

Preemie's dream of flying had come true and he felt wonderful. He could steer, thrust, and spin just like he'd always imagined, and he'd even found the switch for his radio.

*Preemie was so happy, he took a deep breath and shouted, "I'm the king of the universe!"*

His joy was quickly interrupted by a very serious voice.

"Don't tell me, this is your first time in space?" asked Veronica.

Preemie answered sheepishly, "Okay, I won't tell you."

"It's our first time too," said Jeffy.

"Do you know how to land?" asked Veronica.

"I don't know," answered Preemie, "I've never tried."

"Oh no!" said Veronica.

"What are your names?" asked the little rocket, trying to cheer the mood. "I'm Preemie the Explorer."

"Where have you explored?" asked Veronica suspiciously.

*"Umm," said Preemie, thinking as fast as he could. "I've been waiting for the right captain to come along so we could explore together."*

Veronica sat up immediately.

"I'm Captain Veronica," she said confidently. "This is Lola, and the baby over there is Jeffy."

"Hey!" cried Jeffy, looking hurt and embarrassed. "I'm not a baby!"

Jeffy looked up at Preemie's speakers and asked, "Is she really going to be your captain?"

**"You could all be captains?" suggested Preemie. "I'd like to have three captains."**

"Awesome!" said Jeffy excitedly.

Veronica glared at her little brother. She hated the idea of sharing the captaincy, and knew Jeffy wouldn't challenge her if she scared him with an evil stare. Lola, however, couldn't be scared because she giggled whenever Veronica stared at her.

"Hmmpff!" said Veronica. "Take us home now, please!"

"Why? Will your parents be worried about you?" asked Preemie.

"No, they sent us over to Grandma's house to stay the night," said Jeffy.

"So your grandma will be worried?" asked Preemie.

"No, she wasn't home, so we were walking back to our place when the storm hit," Jeffy replied.

*"Great!" said Preemie. "No one will be worried about you and my builders won't be back until morning, so can we explore the universe for a while?"*

"Yes!" replied Jeffy, looking anxiously towards Veronica for her approval. "Can we?"

Veronica reclined comfortably in the captain's chair, pleased she had been given the power to decide.

"As long as I'm captain, I guess I'll allow it for a short time," she said. "You'll have a better chance of landing safely when the storm has passed at home," she told Preemie in a captainly tone.

"Yay!" cried Jeffy.

"Let's party!" yelled Preemie, switching on his radio which played funky space music.

Jeffy and Veronica did the moonwalk while Lola stretched out her arms and legs like a star and spun around on her back.

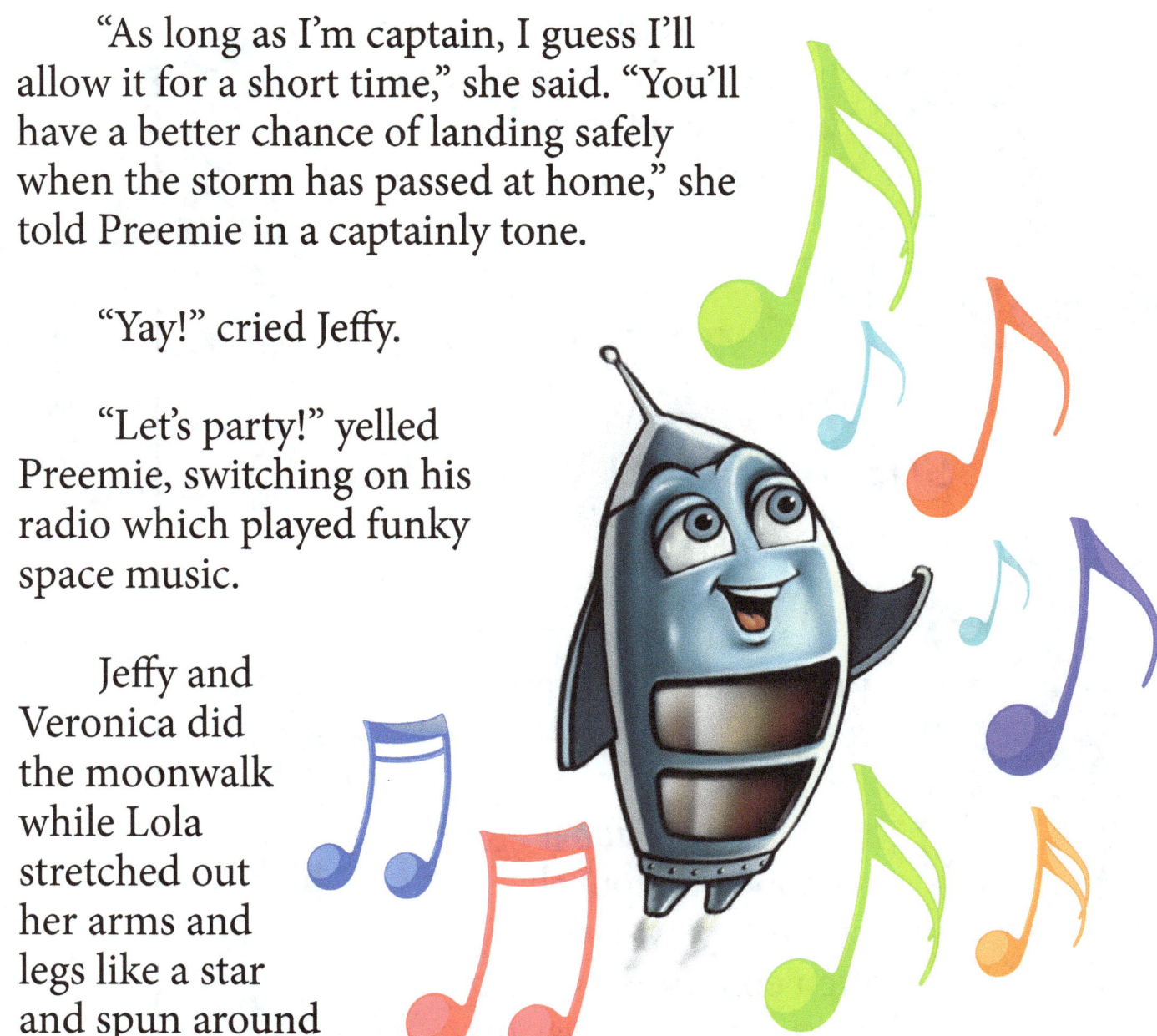

# Chapter 7

Preemie and the children soared joyfully through the twinkling sky, feeling as free as fairies.

All of a sudden, a gang of spaceships and rockets whizzed past with such speed and force, they caused Preemie to tumble and spin like he was caught in a whirlpool. The gang doubled back to find the little rocket still spinning like a top.

"Are you okay? Did we hit you?" asked the green space shuttle, as Preemie looked up at them through dizzy eyes.

*"No wonder we didn't see him," joked the snarly red rocket, "he's a little pygmy!"*

"Can we keep him as a pet?" asked the orange rocket.

"No, we can't!" snapped the purple spaceship, who was often embarrassed that the orange rocket was his cousin.

"Hey guys," said Preemie, "I'm not really a small rocket. I've got awesome turbo thrusters and a big outer shell, and as soon as I get them attached, I will be incredible!"

"Aww, he's even got pygmy passengers," said the orange rocket, looking at the children through Preemie's cabin window.

"They will be old and moldy by the time they get to where they're going!" said the red rocket.

*The gang of spacecraft laughed as a sad, nervous feeling filled Preemie's engines. Preemie's lights dimmed and flickered. Jeffy, Veronica, and Lola watched as the little rocket tried his best to be brave.*

23

*"You don't understand," said Preemie. "I'm supposed to be much bigger, but there was a fierce storm with deafening thunder and crashing lightning which smashed my tower to bits, and the children screamed like crazy so I had to take off—"*

Snnnooooooooorrrrrrreeeeee

Preemie's voice was overpowered by loud snoring coming from the red rocket.

The rest of the gang roared with laughter as the red rocket pretended to wake up startled.

"Oh, I'm sorry," he said sarcastically, "but your story was so interesting, it was the perfect time to take a nap."

Preemie turned away, trying to hide his sadness, but his dimming lights and drooping eyes betrayed him.

"Aww, he's making sad eyes like the puppy-dog-stars," said the orange spaceship. "Why can't we keep him?"

"Because cool gangs don't cruise the universe with pygmies!" replied the purple spaceship. "Isn't that right, Red?"

**"That's right, but maybe we could include him in a game of rocketball," said the red rocket. "He could be the ball!"**

The gang laughed as Preemie closed his eyes in despair.

"I do apologize for my friends," said the green space shuttle. "They are wicked."

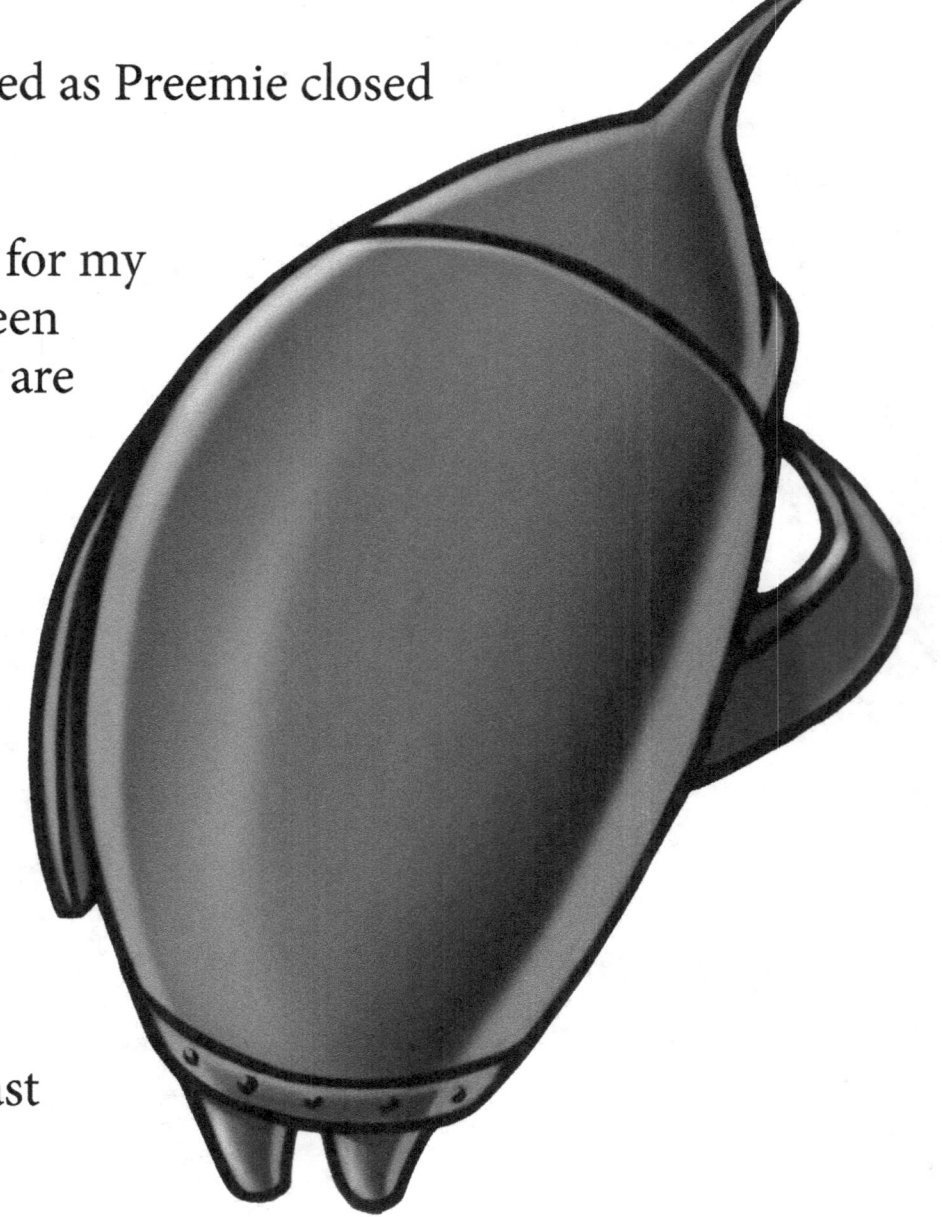

"Yeah, we're wicked!" shouted the other gang members as they playfully pushed and shoved each other.

And, with that, they all flew off as fast as they'd arrived.

# Chapter 8

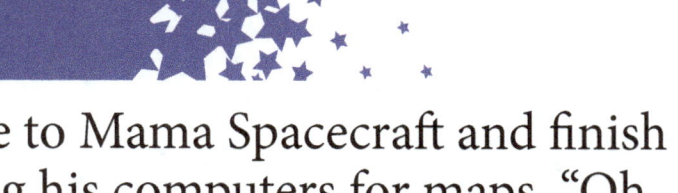

"I've got to go straight home to Mama Spacecraft and finish growing," said Preemie, searching his computers for maps. "Oh, no!" he gasped. "My navigation system isn't connected!"

***"We're lost in space!" said Jeffy. "Cool."***

"Not cool!" cried Preemie. "I should have waited until I was finished! My builders wanted me to be their masterpiece, not a hopeless pygmy."

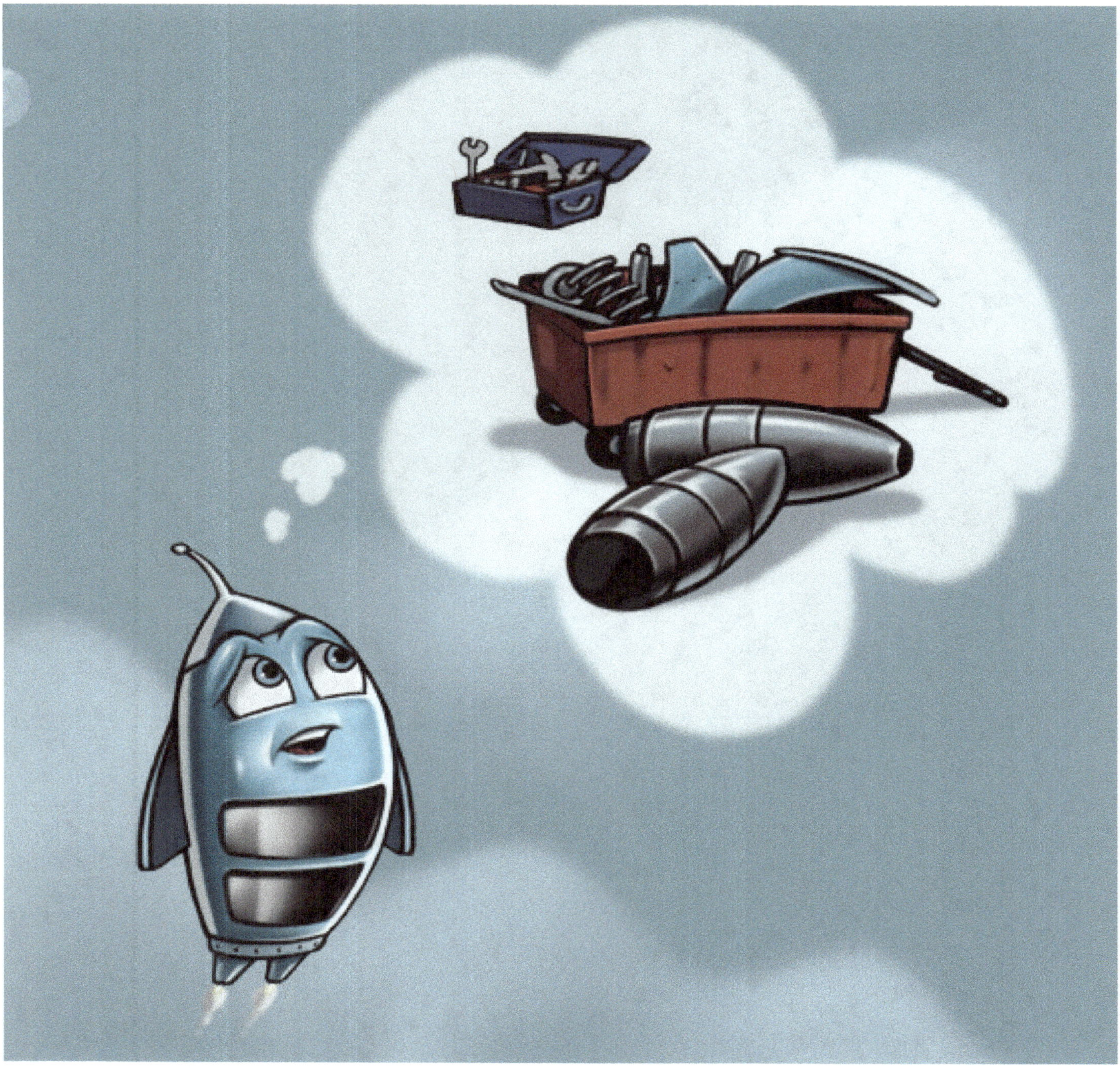

"Don't listen to those mean ships," said Veronica.

## "You saved us from the storm," said Jeffy. "You're our hero."

Preemie appreciated the children's kind words, but he couldn't help feeling upset. He wanted to be like the other spacecraft and fit into their gang. Instead, Preemie just felt lost and confused, and he didn't know what to do.

Tears began welling in his eyes, and his cabin lights faded like a dying candle until they turned off completely.

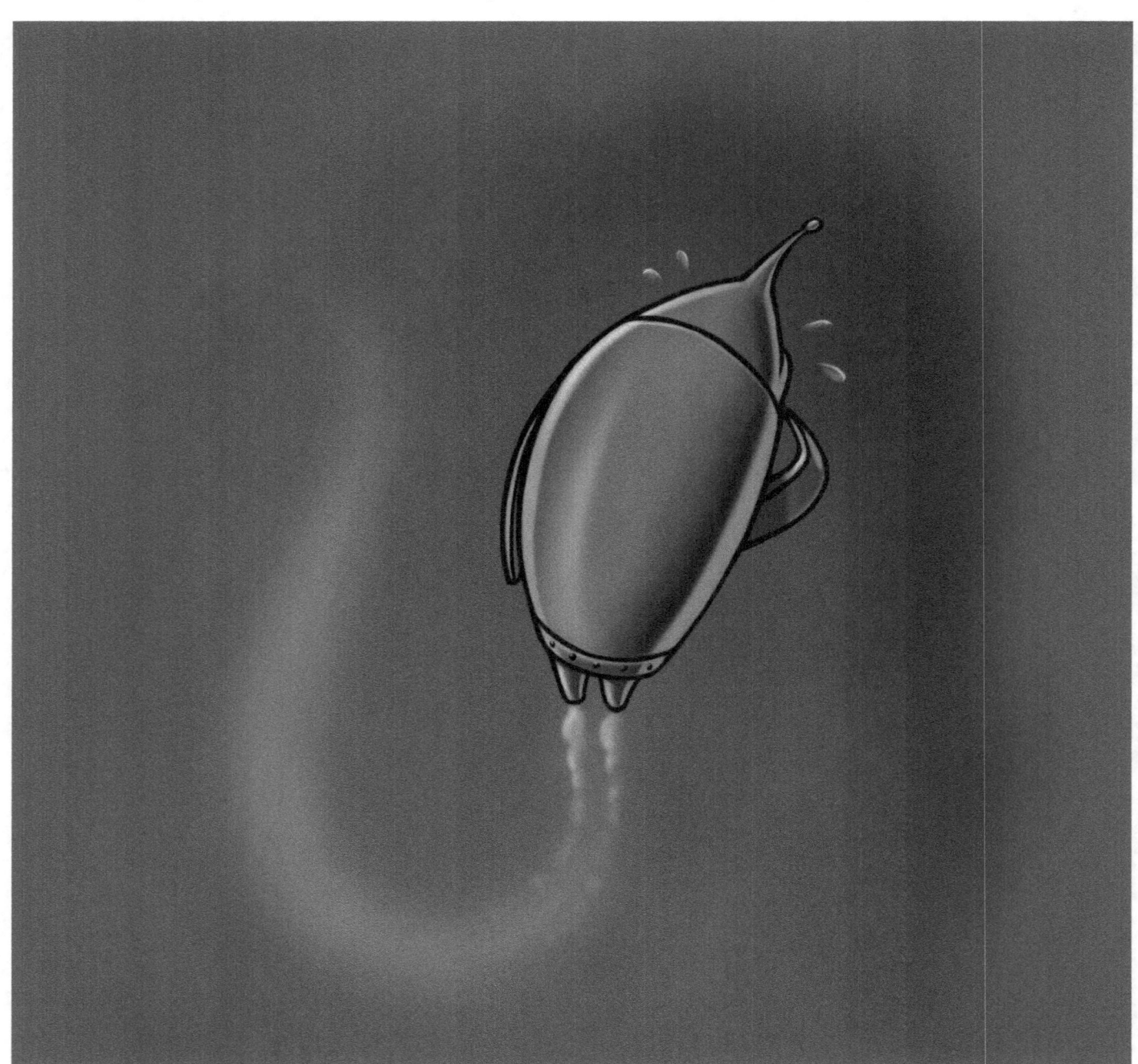

Suddenly, Lola screamed at the top of her lungs. Her high-pitched squeals were much louder than Preemie's gentle sobs.

"What's the matter?" choked the startled little rocket, immediately forgetting his own problems.

"Lola's afraid of the dark," said Veronica.

Preemie switched his cabin lights back on, but Lola's tears continued.

"Too late!" said Jeffy, putting his fingers in his ears. "Only one thing will cheer her up now."

"What is it?" asked Preemie.

"A sand pit!" replied Jeffy and Veronica at the same time.

## "The only way to stop Lola's tears," explained Veronica, "is by letting her build a sandcastle and letting her be the princess."

"Dad says lots of girls go through a princess stage," said Jeffy.

"How do I find a sandpit?" asked Preemie, as Lola howled like a wounded coyote.

"By exploring the universe, I guess!" answered Veronica with a smile.

Jeffy found some plastic knives and forks which he used to make a tiara for Princess Lola. She stopped screaming as Jeffy crowned her, but kept sobbing just enough to make sure no one forgot about the sand pit.

**Preemie's engines revved urgently as he searched the universe. Luckily, they soon found a sandy planet.**

# Chapter 9

Planet NICU was a desert. Sand stretched all the way to the horizon on every side. There were no houses or buildings, just holes in the ground which looked like giant ant nests.

Preemie manoeuvered himself into a landing position. He hovered nervously.

Veronica closed her eyes and mumbled, "Please don't crash, please don't crash, please don't crash..."

As the little rocket lowered himself very gently, Veronica opened one eye just in time to watch his first perfect landing.

"This must be the biggest sandpit in the whole universe," said Jeffy.

In fact, Planet NICU was a special place where tiny babies who had been born too soon were brought from all over the universe to be cared for by moles and kangaroos. Deep inside a network of underground tunnels, the babies slept in enclosed plastic cribs which helped them grow as if they were still inside their mothers' bellies.

*The moles, who were doctors and nurses, treated the babies with special medical procedures.*

*The kangaroos, who were in charge of making the babies feel safe and loved, provided lots of gentle hugs, sways, and lullabies.*

Each medical station was set up near the base of an entrance tunnel to provide easy access from the surface.

Jeffy and Veronica were exploring NICU when they crawled into one of the large surface holes and continued all the way down the sandy burrow until they reached a medical station. The mole on duty was surprised to see the children, but he allowed them to stay.

"Why do you have a hospital down here?" asked Veronica.

"Because it's dark, warm, and quiet which is soothing for the babies," explained the mole.

"Why are those bald mice inside that empty fish tank?" asked Jeffy.

"That's called a humidicrib, and those little animals are a lovely species from the planet, Doop," replied the mole, pointing towards the crib which held the hairless creatures. "A Doopentine is supposed to be as prickly as a grown up porcupine at birth, so these babies still have a lot of growing to do before they can survive above the ground."

"Ooh, imagine giving birth to a prickly Doopentine," said Veronica.

# Chapter 10

Up on the surface, Lola was working hard on her sandcastle while Preemie enjoyed the attention of a caring kangaroo. Preemie's worries floated from his mind as the kangaroo's hugs reminded him of Googie and Tad. It was obvious that kindness and care worked just as well for rockets as they did for people and animals.

"Uhh ba boo boo," said Lola in a demanding tone, drawing Preemie's attention to her impressive building.

Lola was only one year old, but she had a talent for making sandcastles. She had once visited a large amusement park in which fairytale princesses lived in wondrous castles with tall towers and pointed roofs. Lola imagined herself as one of those princesses, and had made her own castles with the same magical qualities she'd seen at the amusement park ever since.

Lola looked at Preemie and pointed to the castle roof. He understood what she wanted and began helping.

To make the castle tall, Preemie needed to transport sand to its rooftops. He worked out how to suck sand into his exhaust pipes and carefully hold it there while flying to the top of the castle. Preemie then thrust the sand out of his exhausts while hovering above the castle roofs.

Lola applauded the little rocket for his cleverness. Preemie also figured out how to shape the castle walls and roofs using his wings and cap. With Lola working on the ground and Preemie working up high, they made a fantastic team.

"Every kingdom in the entire universe will be envious of this magnificent castle, Your Royal Highness," said Preemie with a bow.

# Chapter 11

News of the fantastic sandcastle being built by a baby and a rocket, spread quickly across NICU.

Veronica and Jeffy followed some curious moles and kangaroos who were heading towards the surface to see if the rumours were true.

*Crowded around the castle, they all watched in awe as Preemie lifted Princess Lola to the top of her glorious creation.*

Lola reached out and planted a flagpole in the highest roof as the finishing touch. An eruption of cheers and applause followed.

Lola was so excited, she forgot about being a princess and raised her arms like a rock star. Preemie's headlights shone like sunbeams as he landed gently amongst the crowd.

The moles and kangaroos told Preemie all about the babies who were underground.

"Wow. A planet especially for preemies!" said Preemie. "How do you fix them?"

"The same way you fix anything," said one of the moles, "with care and love. We work on the patients' bodies, and the kangaroos work on their happiness."

"How do hugs, sways, and lullabies keep the babies happy for their whole lives?" asked Jeffy.

*"Kangaroo care shows babies they are perfect just the way nature made them,"* replied a kangaroo.

*"Any creature who knows they're perfect will always find a path to happiness,"* added a mole.

"What if a creature isn't perfect?" asked Preemie. "What if being different means he can't do some of the thngs he's supposed to be able to do, and doesn't fit in with his own kind?"

*"Every creature has strengths and skills that make them perfect in their own way,"* said a kangaroo.

*"You just have to concentrate on the things you're good at, and not worry about what others think of you."*

Preemie glanced at Princess Lola and wondered how she had already learnt these lessons. Even though she was very small and young, she had been able to create an amazing work of art with the sandcastle.

It then occurred to Preemie that he too had been clever and skillful despite being very small and young.

'Pygmies wouldn't usually be able to build and shape high castle roofs,' he thought, smiling to himself.

Suddenly, Preemie heard a whizzing sound coming from the sky. He looked up to see the gang of rockets and spaceships they had met earlier, fast approaching.

# Chapter 12

Preemie watched the gang of spacecraft land. Despite feeling jitters in his fuel tank, Preemie tried to stay calm. He looked towards a kangaroo who reassured him.

*"It's your differences that can make you great,"* said the kangaroo. *"Be happy with yourself just the way you are."*

'Sometimes it's extra hard to be happy with yourself when you're as small as me,' Preemie thought as he timidly looked up at the fearsome red rocket.

A moment later, Veronica pushed past him.

"Don't sweat it," she said, "I've dealt with bullies before."

"I'll be okay," stammered Preemie.

"I know," replied Veronica, "but it's a captain's job to protect her rocket-ship."

Before Preemie could argue, Veronica pointed her finger at the red rocket's face, glared her meanest glare, and yelled, "Listen, Mister, big rockets should not bully little rockets, so play nice!"

The red rocket picked up a trail of stardust which had fallen from a passing comet.

*"I'm not a bully, little girl," he said, "I just want to play my favourite game, 'pin the tail on the pygmy'."*

The red rocket turned towards Preemie, closed his eyes, then poked the dangling trail of stardust towards the little rocket's backside. Preemie ducked and dodged to avoid being 'tailed,' as the red rocket's gang laughed loudly.

Jeffy was so inspired by his sister's courage, he felt a sudden urge to support her in battle.

"Bad guys never win, you know!" Jeffy announced, puffing out his chest like a comic book super-hero and marching heroically forward. He squinted his eyes, tightened his lips, and tried his best to copy Veronica's scary glare.

"He looks like he just sucked a lemon," said the red rocket, smirking at Jeffy.

44

"Aww, don't hurt my pets," said the orange rocket.

"They're not your pets!" snapped the purple spaceship.

"Shhh," said the green space shuttle, wondering what Jeffy was going to say next.

Jeffy stood between his sister and Preemie, clutching one hand and one wing.

"I don't know what a pygmy is," Jeffy said to the red rocket, "but you should be a whole lot nicer when you're talking to an awesome rocket and its awesome captain!"

Veronica smiled proudly, but Preemie lowered his eyes in embarrassment as a roar of laughter rose from the gang of spacecraft.

"Rocket? Are you sure that's not a kid's toy?" answered the red rocket, pointing at Preemie. "He looks like a funny little garden gnome to me. Perhaps you should perch him next to this fairy castle to scare away the mice and birds."

The red rocket looked directly at Jeffy and knocked over one of the castle's magnificent towers. Jeffy's heart thumped with fear, and his stomach filled with nervous butterflies. Veronica could see the panic in Jeffy's eyes as he cowered backwards into the crowd, and she knew his fight was over.

*"Wow! Look how clever you are!" Veronica hollered at the red rocket, distracting him from Jeffy's retreat. "Who would have guessed the big bad bully could knock over a sandcastle all by himself?"*

The gang of spacecraft laughed at Veronica's sarcasm and her confidence grew.

"Aww, did I embarrass you?" continued Veronica. "Look, you're blushing!"

The gang laughed even louder, as their toughest, meanest member squirmed. Veronica strutted up the castle's highest steps to face the red rocket, eye to eye.

"What's the matter tough guy? Run out of stupid comments?" she asked.

The red rocket had never heard the gang laugh at his expense before. He didn't know what to do or say, but Veronica did.

"I think you're angry because no one ever showed you any love," she said.

**Veronica reached up and planted a big sloppy kiss right on the red rocket's lips.**

The gang exploded with laughter and jeering.

"She got you good, Red," said the orange rocket, before making a variety of smoochy, kissing sounds.

The red rocket was speechless. He just stared at Veronica. Deep inside his big red engines, anger bubbled and boiled like a volcano. He snarled and gnashed his teeth. His eyes bulged from their sockets as if his head was about to explode. Suddenly, he shot into the sky.

Tee Hee

Ba ha ha ha

He he he

# Chapter 13

"Oh, no! Crazy missile on the loose," announced the purple spaceship as the red rocket flew wildly across the sky.

"Aww, I love it when Red goes mental," chortled the orange rocket.

The red rocket began looping and twisting madly. He zoomed past the crowd so closely that the sandcastle shook.

"Why is he doing that?" Veronica asked nervously.

*"He's showing off," said the green space shuttle. "Red is a very proud rocket, and you made him feel like a fool. Now he's trying to prove how clever he really is."*

"He is proving something, but it isn't cleverness," said a mole, putting Lola safely into a kangaroo's pouch.

'Maybe the red rocket could use some kangaroo care,' thought Preemie.

The red rocket lost control of his acrobatic turns. He spun crazily in every direction before crashing into one side of the sandcastle.

"Bullseye!" yelled the orange rocket.

"That's not a bullseye," argued the purple spaceship. "Half the castle is still standing!"

The red rocket picked himself up and spat sand from between his teeth. He frowned menacingly, then glared down furiously at Veronica who was now being shielded by Preemie's wing. The moles and kangaroos begged the red rocket to calm down.

# Chapter 14

After a few frightening minutes, the red rocket turned and flew a short distance away. Everyone breathed a sigh of relief except Veronica.

"What happens when the red rocket's showing off doesn't work?" asked Veronica as she hurried inside Preemie's cabin and hid behind the captain's chair.

"Red doesn't like to give up until he's made his point," answered the purple spaceship.

The red rocket fixed his sights directly on Preemie as if he was taking aim. Then, like a catapulting comet, the red rocket launched himself at full speed.

Preemie stared in disbelief as the big angry rocket barrelled towards him. Veronica screamed and Preemie blasted himself out of the red rocket's flight path just in time to avoid being crushed like a tin can. The moles and kangaroos gasped.

*"Relax," said the green space shuttle. "Red is an excellent actor. He's just pretending to be a crazy maniac."*

The red rocket turned around and came hammering back towards Preemie and Veronica. This time he was yelling, "I'm going to make baby rocket salad for dinner!"

The moles and kangaroos trembled.

"See, he's even making silly jokes about baby rocket salad," said the green space shuttle with a fake cheery smile, but no one believed the red rocket was acting.

*Preemie turned to Jeffy and Lola who were being guarded by kangaroos. "Don't worry," he said, "I'll look after Veronica. It's a rocket-ship's job to protect his captain."*

Then, with a big puff of exhaust smoke, Preemie disappeared.

# Chapter 15

Preemie flew into the open sky as fast as he could, but the red rocket was soon bumping him from behind, trying to send the little rocket into a tail spin.

*"Go faster!" yelled Veronica.*

*"This is as fast as I go," Preemie replied, wishing he had turbo thrusters.*

"Move then!" ordered Veronica.

Preemie began swerving from side to side, rolling and twisting like a rollercoaster, but he couldn't get away from the red rocket.

Preemie tensed his engines, then spun hard into a sweeping backflip. Veronica hung upside down in her chair as she watched the red rocket fly right underneath her. Preemie was flying beautifully, but he was no match for the speed of the red rocket who was right on his tail again in a matter of moments.

*"First I'm going to squish you, then I'm going to pound you into a frisbee,"* said the red rocket.

"We're doomed," said Veronica, slouching in her chair. "You're just too little and slow."

"I'm sorry," said Preemie.

The red rocket laughed like an evil villain, then swiped Preemie's tail sideways, sending the little rocket into a spin.

"Help!" yelled Preemie as he tumbled through space, trying to regain control.

"Straighten up," ordered Veronica, but Preemie's engines suddenly stalled and he lost all power.

"Oh, no!" cried Veronica as they plummeted towards the surface of NICU.

*"He's going to crash!" yelled the purple spaceship who was watching from the ground with the others.*

Just meters from NICU's surface, Preemie realised he wasn't going to stop in time.

All he could do was flip himself into a vertical position so his nose was pointing straight down.

"I can't watch," said the green space shuttle, using his wing to cover Jeffy's eyes.

The entire crowd held its breath as Preemie reached NICU's surface at full speed. There was no crash, however. Instead, Preemie disappeared straight into one of the holes in the ground.

**"Wow, this is better than T.V.," said the orange rocket.**

Before the crowd had time to sigh with relief, the red rocket came hurtling towards the same hole.

"This may be a tight fit!" said the green space shuttle.

At the last moment, the red rocket swerved sharply and screeched to a stop. He noticed his gang watching, and was annoyed that Preemie and Veronica had, once again, delighted the crowd. The red rocket snarled with frustration, then blasted himself into the hole to resume the chase.

# Chapter 16

Preemie re-started his engines and switched on his headlights as he fell towards the network of underground tunnels.

*"Be careful! The babies, moles, and kangaroos will be just up ahead," said Veronica, reminding Preemie that each medical station was set up near the base of an entrance tunnel.*

Preemie slowed down as the tunnel branched off sideways in three directions. The moles and kangaroos screamed as the little rocket accidentally turned towards the medical station and just managed to avoid crashing into the baby cribs.

"Sorry," yelled Preemie as he spun around and darted off in the opposite direction.

"We've got to get out of here!" said Veronica.

Preemie nodded.

The red rocket soon reappeared. Veronica watched him speed furiously towards them.

"Watch out!" she yelled.

"Yeouch," cried Preemie, as the red rocket smashed him from behind.

"Okay, get ready to make a really sharp turn up ahead," Veronica instructed Preemie.

As they approached an intersecting tunnel, Veronica suddenly yelled, "Now!" and Preemie flung himself around the corner without slowing down. The red rocket had no warning of the change of direction, so he flew straight past the intersection. Being too big to turn around inside the tunnel, the red rocket could not continue the chase.

"Have we lost him?" asked Preemie.

*"Rockets are like sharks, they can't go backwards," said Veronica, "so we've lost him for now."*

"Brilliant. Great thinking, Captain!" said Preemie.

"He will definitely keep looking for us, though," warned Veronica.

Preemie saw a medical station up ahead and stopped beside the baby cribs.

Preemie gazed at the little bundles who were clutching to life with all their might. Their miniature bodies looked so fragile, Preemie felt an instant urge to protect them.

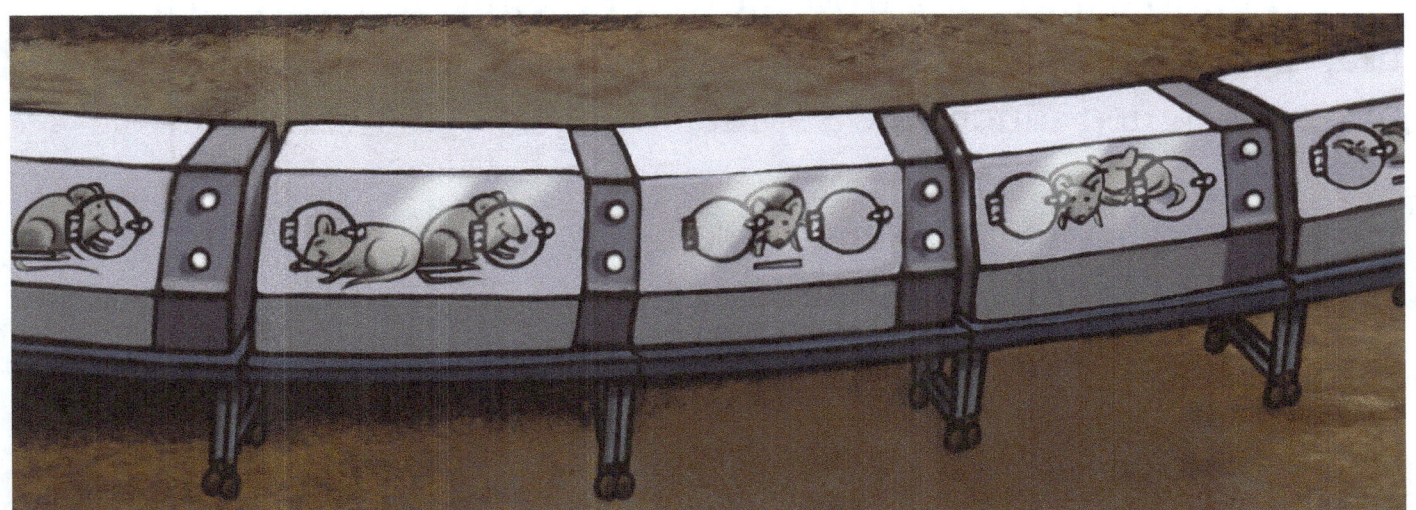

*'So small but so precious,' he thought.*

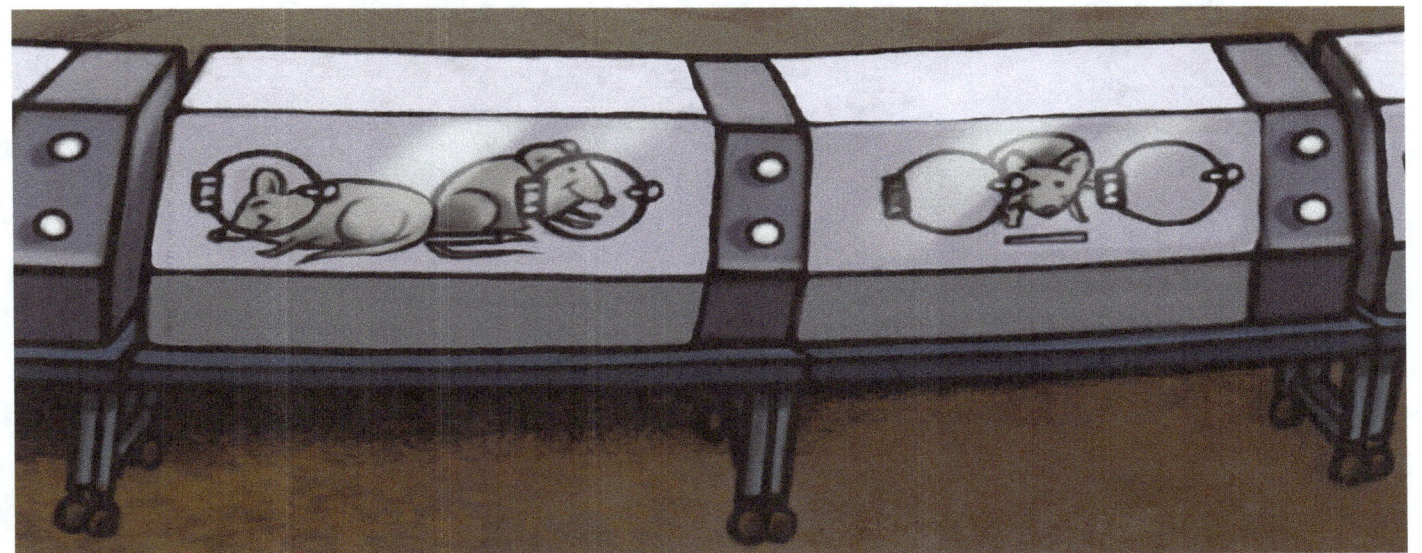

Preemie and Veronica told the mole and kangaroo at the medical station about their chase with the red rocket.

"We're sorry for putting you and the babies in danger," said Veronica. "We didn't mean to come down into your tunnels, and I promise we're going to leave right now."

"You don't have to leave," said the mole. "Luckily, there is a way we can all be safe."

# Chapter 17

The mole and kangaroo showed Preemie and Veronica a map of the underground tunnel network. It was a large circular maze, designed much like a spider web.

"There are no dead-ends or corners in which to get trapped," said the kangaroo. "You'll be safer here in the tunnels than out in the open sky."

"How do we avoid the medical stations?" asked Veronica.

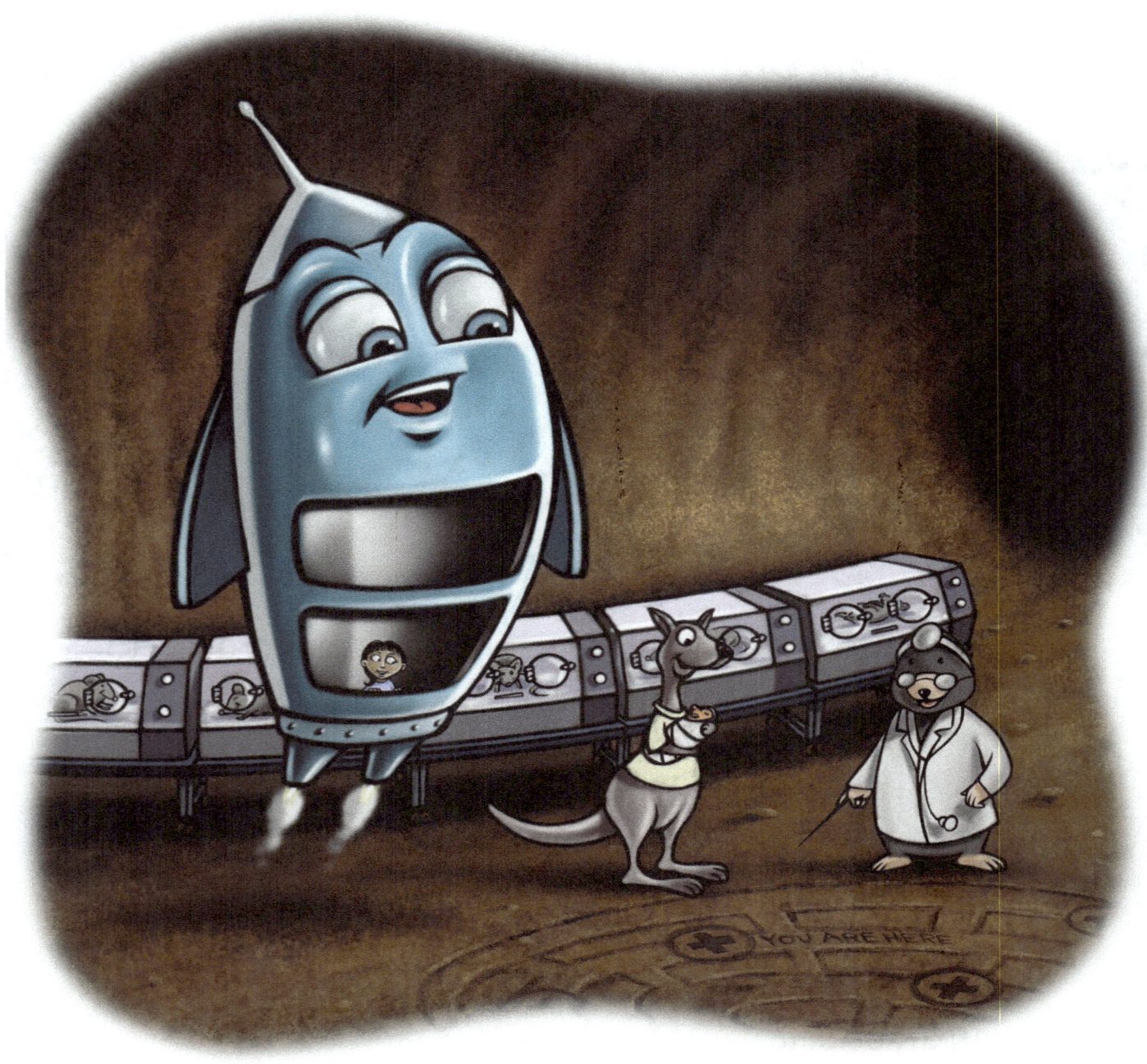

"The north west quarter of the maze is empty," explained the mole, pointing at the map with a stick. "If you stay in that section and keep moving, no one will get hurt."

"Great," said Veronica. "Let's go."

Preemie's thoughts had drifted from the conversation, and he was gazing at the tiny babies in the plastic cribs.

"I wonder if they know how perfect they are," he said to Veronica.

Veronica smiled and wondered the same thing about Preemie.

"Of course they know," she said. "Kangaroo care shows every baby they're perfect, and who wouldn't believe a kangaroo!"

Preemie nodded thoughtfully.

"Now, we better get out of here in case 'Big Red' shows up," Veronica added urgently.

Preemie crept quietly away from the medical station. He turned slowly around the first corner and came face to face with the red rocket who was looking angrier than a bear caught in a trap.

"Uh, oh," stammered Preemie.

"Well this certainly changes the mood," said Veronica.

A vicious engine roar was the red rocket's reply. Preemie spun around and took off like a scared rabbit.

"Head towards the north west," said Veronica.

"My compass doesn't work," said Preemie.

Veronica pointed in the direction the mole had instructed.

"That way!" she said. "Make lots of sharp turns and this bully doesn't stand a chance of catching us."

Veronica was right. Because Preemie was smaller, he could turn much faster in the narrow tunnels. When the red rocket caught up to them, Preemie would dart off in a different direction and get a safe distance away. In fact, the red rocket learnt not to get too close for fear of missing a turn and losing them again.

After a while, Preemie and Veronica felt so safe, they began teasing the red rocket. Preemie would slow down, allowing the red rocket to catch up, then Veronica would press her face against the cabin window and make loud fart noises while drooling like a slobbery dog. Laughing hysterically, Preemie would quickly zip off down another tunnel to escape any punishment. They did this for a long time until Preemie and Veronica were laughing so hard, they didn't notice they were heading straight towards a medical station.

"Watch out!" yelled Veronica, finally spotting the frightened moles and kangaroos who were watching them approach. "Head back to the north west," she said.

Preemie looked for an intersecting tunnel up ahead but there wasn't one. He glanced behind and saw the red rocket zeroing in on them, fast.

**There was nowhere left to turn.**

# Chapter 18

Preemie and Veronica were trapped. The red rocket smirked with delight, realizing he had finally won.

"Any ideas?" Preemie asked Veronica.

"You could squeeze past the medical station," she said, "but if 'Big Red' followed, he would squash everything, including the..."

Veronica couldn't finish her sentence. Thinking of all the damage the red rocket would cause if he tried to fly past the medical station was just too horrible.

"We can't risk it," said Preemie.

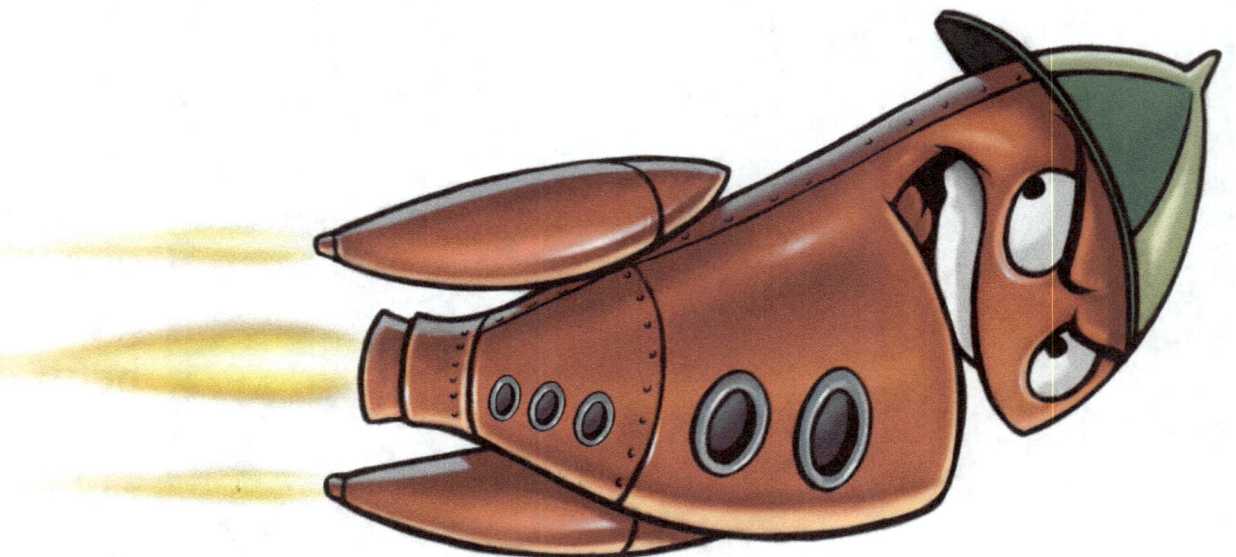

Preemie faced the red rocket and prepared himself for a beating. The red rocket didn't waste any time. He used the pointy tip of his cap to thump Preemie's cabin window, throwing the little rocket off balance.

"Your luck has finally run out, little mouse!" said the red rocket.

Preemie edged backwards, afraid another blow from the red rocket's steel cap might smash his window all over Veronica.

"We only stopped to protect the medical centre," said Veronica.

The red rocket sniggered.

"Those babies are safe now," he said, "but you're not!"

*The red rocket bumped Preemie even harder, and Veronica felt a shiver of fear shoot up her back as she fell to the floor of the cabin.*

Looking up from her crouched position, Veronica saw something that made her fear disappear.

"Remember how each medical station is near an entrance tunnel?" Veronica whispered to Preemie.

Preemie murmured quietly, "Uh huh."

"Well, entrance tunnels go both ways," said Veronica, "and there's one above us right now."

Preemie could hardly believe their luck. The red rocket had unwittingly pushed him right underneath an escape route.

Preemie looked the red rocket in the eye and smiled.

*"Little mice usually feel safe in their holes,"* he said, *"but the universe is calling, 'fly to me rocket, take off and fly to me!'"*

Veronica giggled. The red rocket looked confused. Preemie fired his engines and shot straight up the exit tunnel, aiming for the sky. The red rocket cursed, then followed.

Veronica and Preemie noticed the tunnel getting narrower as they approached the surface.

"You might need to suck in your tummy," Veronica told Preemie as they got closer to the white light of the exit hole.

"I'll make it through," Preemie replied, "but I'm not sure about 'Big Red.'"

*As Preemie flew out into bright sunshine, he and Veronica heard the brutal crunching of steel as the red rocket's body smashed against the side of the tunnel. The noise slowed like an old steam train grinding to a halt, until the red rocket was motionless, stuck tight between the tunnel walls, with just his sideways cap and angry face poking out into the sunlight.*

# Chapter 19

Veronica danced around the cabin, laughing and singing, as Preemie soared safely across the sky above NICU.

*"Let him bake in the sun like a hot potato,"* said Veronica, pointing down at the red rocket who was stuck in the hole, tighter than a cork in a bottle.

Preemie headed back towards the red rocket.

"Are we going to tease him some more?" asked Veronica. "Maybe we should teach him some manners!" she said.

Preemie landed and Veronica got out.

"You were saved by this stupid tunnel," said the red rocket.

"Don't blame the tunnel," said Veronica. "It was you being stupid that saved us."

Preemie didn't say anything. He just stared at the powerful, ferocious red rocket who had become as helpless as a caged lion. Preemie's lights dimmed a little.

*Preemie wondered what the moles and kangaroos would do if they were in the same situation. Then, without the others even noticing, he took off, leaving Veronica and the red rocket to their bickering.*

"Your builders must have been evil to give you such a nasty brain," said Veronica.

"Rockets have computers, not brains!" answered the red rocket. "And you call me stupid!" he scoffed.

"Well, good luck using your computers to get out of that hole," Veronica replied as she walked away.

"Hey," yelled the red rocket, hoping Veronica wouldn't leave him there alone. "You're nasty too!"

Veronica turned around.

"I'm just standing up for my family against a bully," she said.

"You bully your little brother," said the red rocket.

"I do not!" replied Veronica, crossing her arms.

"Be honest! You order him around like you're his boss!" said the red rocket.

Veronica huffed, wondering how the red rocket knew she was sometimes a bit forceful when helping Jeffy make decisions.

"I do what big sisters are supposed to do," she said. "I teach him how things are!"

"Ahh," said the red rocket, "you teach him that older sisters are allowed to boss and bully their younger brothers because that's how things are, right?"

"No! I'm a good sister!" snapped Veronica, getting very annoyed. "You don't know anything about my family!"

The red rocket paused, then replied in a gentle tone.

"I don't know your family, but I do know about bullying," he said, "and I've seen a look in your brother's eyes which shows me that he sometimes feels a lot smaller on the inside than he appears on the outside. Do you understand what that means?"

"Yes, it means he's terrified of you!" said Veronica.

"No," said the red rocket. "Only someone he really admires could make him feel sad like that. You're his hero, you know?"

Veronica looked surprised, then scowled at the red rocket.

"Oh I get it! Now you're stuck in a hole, you're pretending to be all sensitive and caring!" she grumbled. "Well, I don't believe it! As if you'd know or care about how it feels to be bullied!"

The red rocket was silent. Veronica peered deep into his eyes and saw the same look he had just described seeing in Jeffy's eyes. She suddenly realized the red rocket did understand the pain of being bullied which was the reason he was so angry all the time.

# Chapter 20

A loud bang interrupted the quiet moment between the red rocket and Veronica.

"Ouch!" said the red rocket, who knew exactly where the sound had come from.

*It was Preemie. He had found his way back into the tunnel and was bumping the red rocket's tail, trying to push him out of the hole.*

A muffled voice came from the underground. "Veronica, start digging."

"Preemie?" Veronica replied loudly. "I know your computers are not all connected so perhaps you've forgotten that this big red brute just tried to pound you into a frisbee!"

Preemie didn't answer, but Veronica could hear him continuing to work down in the tunnel. She sat silently on the peak of the red rocket's cap, and listened for a while.

"Well, of all the crazy things that have happened today, this would have to be the craziest!" Veronica finally said as she got up and started to dig the red rocket free from his hole.

It wasn't long before the red rocket could wiggle his engines and tail.

"Try thrusting out now," yelled Preemie, as Veronica cleared the area.

*The red rocket's engines rumbled and roared as he lurched out of the hole and blasted into the sky. Preemie and Veronica watched as the red rocket looped and spun like a playful dolphin. A wonderful feeling filled Preemie's body, and he realized he didn't need an outer shell and turbo thrusters to feel proud of himself.*

"Do you think we should get out of here before he remembers he's an angry bully?" asked Veronica.

Preemie thought for a moment.

"Let's stay and see if he forgets," he replied.

# Chapter 21

To celebrate his escape from the hole, the red rocket used his exhaust fumes to write, 'I'm Free', in big fancy letters across the sky. He then returned to Preemie and Veronica, and hovered over them, glaring down like a scary school teacher.

*In a deep, serious voice, the red rocket bellowed, "It's finally time you two got what you deserved!"*

"I told you we shouldn't have helped him," Veronica said to Preemie. "Once a bully, always a bully!"

"And, what you deserve is an apology and a thank-you," continued the red rocket, changing his tone mid-sentence.

Preemie and Veronica smiled with relief.

"Thank you for helping me out of the tunnel, and sorry for being stupid and nasty," said the red rocket in a quiet, sincere tone.

"I'm sorry I've been so horrible too," said Veronica. "I feel terrible about it now."

"I think bullying makes everyone feel bad," said the red rocket, "especially the bully."

Veronica agreed.

"Sorry for teasing you in the tunnels," added Preemie.

**"You were amazing in the tunnels,"** replied the red rocket. **"I never realized being small could make you go faster, but in the tunnels, you were kicking my butt!"**

Preemie beamed with pride.

"Then he kicked your butt right out of the tunnel," said Veronica.

"You should come and fly with my gang?" said the red rocket.

"Thanks, but I wouldn't be able to keep up," said Preemie. "I need to get back to Mama Spacecraft so my builders can finish me."

"Do you know the way to Earth?" asked Veronica. "We're lost!"

The red rocket smiled warmly.

"I'll do you a deal," he said. "Come and explore the universe with us this afternoon, and we'll get you home by dinner time."

Preemie's lights lit up again. Veronica squealed with excitement.

"Let's tell Jeffy and Lola," said Preemie.

# Chapter 22

Back at the sandcastle, Jeffy and Lola were eating lunch and enjoying kangaroo rides around Lola's kingdom.

Veronica thanked the moles and kangaroos for their kindness. Preemie thanked them for their wise advice.

**"The gift of wisdom is only useful if it is properly unwrapped," replied a mole, "and you unwrapped it all by yourself."**

The red rocket told his gang that Preemie and the children were going to join them for the afternoon.

"You made friends with the pygmy?" asked the purple spaceship.

The red rocket nodded. "Who'd have thought cruising with a pygmy could be so awesome?" he said.

"See, Red really is just a big softy," said the green space shuttle, winking at the kangaroos and moles.

"Hello, pet," said the orange rocket. "Can we build sandcastles together?"

Preemie smiled and nodded.

"For the last time," insisted the purple spaceship, "he's not our pet!"

"No," added the red rocket. "He's one of us!"

Preemie revved his engines as the children prepared for take off.

"You take the captain's chair," Veronica said to Jeffy.

"Really?" said Jeffy, his eyes shining with excitement.

"We should all be captains," replied Veronica.

Jeffy leapt into the captain's chair, then changed his mind. Veronica watched as Jeffy picked up Lola and buckled her into the captain's chair instead.

*"If we're all captains, they're all captain's chairs," he said, "but Lola will like this one because it spins."*

The children waved goodbye to the moles and kangaroos.

"Let's have some fun," yelled the red rocket.

Hoots, cheers, whistles, and yells were heard right across the universe as Preemie and the gang shot into the sky, leaving NICU far behind.

# Chapter 23

Preemie and the children were soon honorary gang members. Their new friends; Red, Orange, Green, and Purple showed them many strange and wonderful planets and stars.

Jeffy's favorite was Sirius, the dog star, who chased balls and begged for treats.

Veronica loved 'Planet Picture' which was made of many electronic screens that all changed image at the same time, so the planet could look like a giant basketball, then transform into a snowfield, or an ocean, or anything else you can imagine.

Lola loved being part of the games Preemie played with the other spacecraft. She cheered and clapped as Preemie won at 'hide and seek' because he was able to hide behind even the smallest meteoroids. Preemie also won the game, 'catch the asteroid,' because he could dart in and out between tight clusters of stars and catch his prize more easily than his larger friends.

*"I'll never make fun of another pygmy,"* said Red, shaking stardust off his cap after crashing into three stars. Preemie smiled at his new best friend.

# Chapter 24

Green let the children use his computer phone to call their parents.

"Dad, we're in outer space with our very own rocket called Preemie, and we've made friends with a gang of colored spacecraft," said Jeffy enthusiastically.

"That's great, Son. Remember to help Grandma with the washing up. We'll see you for dinner tomorrow night."

"But, Dad, didn't you hear me? We're in outer space."

"That sounds exciting, Son. Oh, and don't drink from the cup in the bathroom because Grandma leaves her false teeth in there. Your mother sends her love. Have fun. Bye."

"He didn't believe me!" said Jeffy, hanging up the phone.

Veronica gave Jeffy a warm sisterly hug.

"Maybe he didn't believe you because last time you called from Grandma's, you told him there were dinosaurs in the kitchen," she said.

"There were dinosaurs in the kitchen," insisted Jeffy.

"Lizards aren't dinosaurs," replied Veronica.

**"I think lizards are little dinosaurs!"** said Jeffy with a growl in his voice. "They might be smaller but they're just as awesome."

Preemie smiled because he agreed with Jeffy.

# Chapter 25

The children asked if they could stay in space for the night because their parents weren't worried. Preemie and the gang loved the idea. They all roasted marshmallows on a little flaming star until the children were too tired to keep their eyes open.

**Preemie watched as the children drifted off to sleep. He felt very lucky that they had found him during that terrible storm.**

Jeffy and Veronica had helped Preemie find the courage to survive the journey into space and the bullying from the larger spacecraft.

Little Lola had led Preemie to NICU where she showed him that amazing achievements are possible no matter how small or different he may be. The wise moles and kangaroos had explained why:

*"Everyone is great at something. Sometimes it just takes a while to figure out what it is."*

Preemie realized he had even learnt some lessons from the red rocket. Red's bullying had allowed Preemie to discover his own bravery. When Red got stuck in the tunnel, Preemie discovered that being forgiving and helpful feels much better than holding a grudge. Finally, when Red became friendly, Preemie learnt that kindness can be contagious.

# Chapter 26

"You know, I was never really ready to fly," Preemie confessed to the other spacecraft before telling them about his builders' plans for him and his emergency take-off.

"I can't imagine you being big with turbo thrusters and an outer shell," said Red. "You're so great at being small and zippy."

"I agree," said Green. "Stay the way you are. Red is proof that bigger is not always better!"

Everyone chuckled, including Red.

"My builders wanted me to be their masterpiece," said Preemie. "They said when I was perfect, they would paint:

across my window."

Green quickly produced some paints and brushes, and within minutes Preemie was proudly wearing his name and title, painted in all the glorious colors of the rainbow.

## *"Aww, you're perfect now," said Orange, and everyone agreed.*

Preemie's lights shone brighter than the sun.

"I can't sleep when you're so happy!" grumbled Veronica.

"Sorry," said Preemie, dimming his lights to a faint glow.

*They all laughed and, as funky space music gently soothed the children in their sleep, Preemie and the gang moon-danced the night away.*